THE GLOBAL FELLOWSHIP

PRELUDE TO THE INFINITUS SAGA

CHRISTIANE JOY ALLISON

Allison Publishing

Wasilla, AK

Allison
Publishing

www.AllisonPublishing.com

© Christiane Joy Allison, 2019
Edited by Joy Anne Vaughn
Cover Art by Brandon Moore

Allison Publishing
PO Box 877945
Wasilla, AK 99687
AllisonPublishing.AK@gmail.com

Library of Congress Control Number: 2019910673

Names: Allison, Christiane Joy, author.
Title: The global fellowship : prelude to The infinitus saga / Christiane
    Allison.
Description: Wasilla, AK : Allison Publishing, [2019]
Identifiers: ISBN 9781733844604 (paperback) | ISBN 9781733844611 (Kindle)
    | ISBN 9781733844628 (ePub) | ISBN 9781733844635 (PDF)
Subjects: LCSH: Imaginary societies--Fiction. | Client/server computing—
    Social aspects--Fiction. | Teenagers with disabilities--Fiction. | Brothers
    and sisters--Fiction. | Survival--Fiction. | LCGFT: Science fiction. |
    Novellas.
Classification: LCC PS3601.L4477 G56 2019 (print) | LCC PS3601.L4477
    (ebook) | DDC 813/.6--dc23

To my family, who make me stronger than my body.

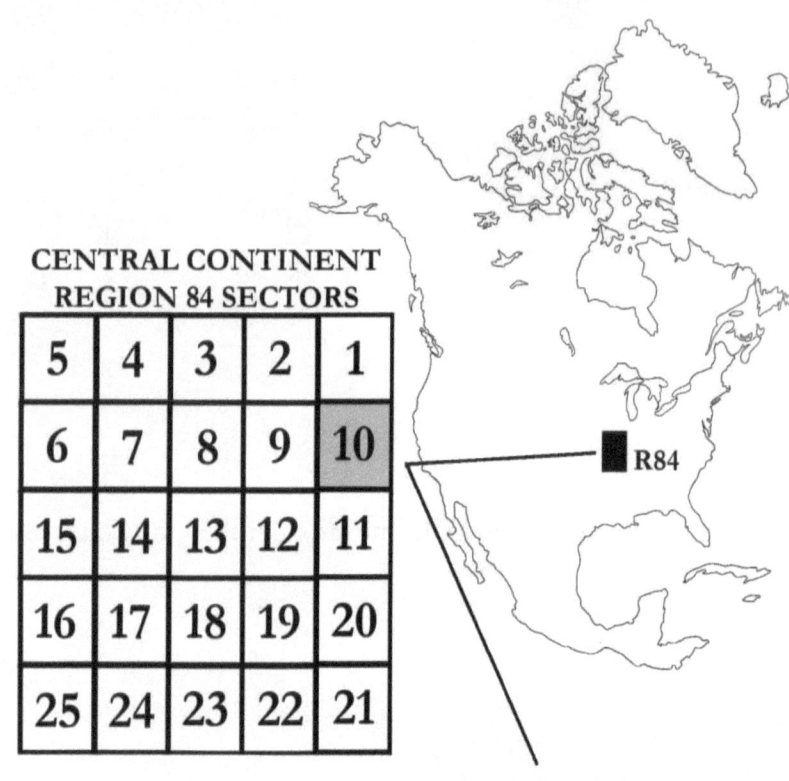

CENTRAL CONTINENT REGION 84 SECTORS

5	4	3	2	1
6	7	8	9	10
15	14	13	12	11
16	17	18	19	20
25	24	23	22	21

R84

SECTOR 10 DISTRICTS

E	D	C	B	A
F	G	H	I	J
P	N	M	L	K
Q	R	S	T	U
Z	Y	X	W	V

THE DREGS —

CHAPTER
1

They'll never see this coming! Well, Gina might, but not Mom and—

A crash of twisting metal and breaking glass echoes outside my window and my finger draws a huge smudge through the monstrous creature's right leg.

"Dammit." I shouldn't have done the shading in the same layer. I start to toss the easel aside but force myself to slow down and take a deep breath—tech this old can break easy.

I'm lucky Gina, found this one intact a few months ago. She should have sold it with the other off-GRID workstations she'd scrounged, but she gave it to me. She could've found a buyer. Being able to draw into a computer using only my hands is a pretty wicked concept for something so primitive.

What the hell was that, anyway?

Setting the easel down carefully, my bed railing creaks a complaint as I pull myself upright. That crash sounded bad but kind of muted. It must have come from a couple blocks away. There's still a maintained road that close in District T, so it could have been an autobus or drone. I'd worry about squids, but that sounded more like a collision than an explosion.

Jeez, I wonder if anyone's hurt? Some of the shirkers near the barrel fires below my window begin shouting back and forth. A clear, soft siren's wail adds itself to the commotion.

Stumbling to the window, I grab the sill and hang on tight to keep from falling as the blood leaves my head and my eyesight dims. A dull headache starts as my heart pounds loudly in my ears. It passes in seconds like it always does, so I stick my head out the open window to try and see what's going on.

Hosni is jogging with Byron and Meadow up the street toward District T. The little girl is slung on Hosni's back atop his short, bony frame while her brother races ahead. They and a couple of guys I don't know leave the burn barrels and run right past Crazy Rob.

Man, you can tell nothing interesting ever happens around here.

Rob is staying carefully close to the buildings and ducking into every hiding place. I chuckle a little as he slips behind an old shipping crate. Mom always says to mind my manners, but it's stupid funny that Crazy Rob thinks they're after him. He's got nothing the Community would want. He's in more danger of the people around here grabbing his stash of MREs.

Gina says he messes up the Community's GRIDtech when he's around, but that's just another one of his stories. He's got enough of those for someone with two lifetimes. But as Dad always reminds me, he's harmless, and he helps out sometimes. We're poor enough he must've decided we're not *Community spies*.

After he disappears, the street returns to the boring hum of normal activity. Old Yeon-Jae is hanging some clothes on a line and occasionally scolding some of the little kids whose parents must've run off to check out the noise. One of the new guys is manning the barrel fires. Gina hasn't found out what his name is yet.

The ache in my legs intensifies steadily as I stand until it's gnawing its way into my bones. I'll head back to bed and leave the window open so I can hear when news comes back to the camp below. On the way, I pour myself a cup of warm water from the glass jug by the door. Damn, it's almost out. Soon I'll have to refill it from one of the rain barrels outside and lug it back up those freakin' stairs. No way I can manage that right now. I'm already trembling too much. I drop back down into my nest of pillows and blankets on the musty old mattress Dad found at the recycling center.

Mom and Dad left this morning before I woke up, but I don't remember who they were meeting. Gina went out to close a tech deal about an hour ago. When they get home, I'll ask if they saw what happened.

I stare at the diagram I've made on the wall; above the chess game I'm playing with Mom. I think I've finally worked out the plot and stats for the upcoming battle, but even though I'm the DM, it's hard to keep Gina from outmaneuvering my characters. I hope I can get the creature fully colored-in before the game tomorrow night. Mom's been trying to peek, but I think I've managed to keep it out of sight.

I hate that I can't help support the family, but Mom says family fun is important too. Without me and her, I swear Dad and Gina would never take a break or stop to enjoy anything. So, I pick my easel back up and start to work on fixing the smudge.

An hour later, I make a new freakin' smudge when Crazy Rob starts pounding like the devil on my door. "Arthur!" he shouts. "Arthur, are you in there?"

"What?" I yell back, setting the easel aside again. Thank God I started a new layer this time. "What is it?" I'd stopped paying attention, but now it's obvious the commotion has returned to camp, and Crazy Rob is looking for a new person to tell the story to.

"Arthur, where's Gina?"

Huh? I punch in the codes for my door locks on the pad next to my bed and it pops open.

"I don't know where she is." I struggle to sit back up. "Why?"

When he shoves the door open—holy shit!—he looks ten times as crazy as normal. His eyes are wide and red-rimmed, and my heartbeat accelerates. He always, always wears a Faraday stocking cap, but it's now stuffed in his pocket and his hair is sticking up in all directions. He's coated in sweat, huffing and puffing like he ran the whole way back.

"I need to talk to you and Gina." He shuffles over to the window to glance down at the camp. "Where is she?"

"I told you, I don't—"

"I'm right here," Gina shouts from the hallway. "Rob, what's wrong?" When she comes inside, she's wearing the tank top and shorts she usually sleeps in. Her feet are bare. Her sleek, auburn hair is wet, so she must have been cleaning up in the rain-catch barrels outside.

"When did you get home?" I ask.

"Like fifteen minutes ago. I went straight to wash up. But everybody—"

A scream from outside makes Gina bolt over to look down at the street, but Rob grabs her by the shoulders to pull her back. Watch it, man!

"What the hell is going on?" Using adrenaline to jump up, I put myself between them—leaning against Gina briefly until the blood returns to my face. At well over six feet, I loom over him but feeling faint ruins the intimidation factor.

"Gina. Arthur." He backs up with a sigh. "I need you to both sit down for a minute."

I watch the color drain from Gina's face in an instant. She glances at me and then glances back toward the window. "Rob, you're scaring me. Everybody's going crazy out there. Somebody said something about a crash?"

"I know sweetheart." He gestures to the bed with pain in his eyes and I sit down on the mattress again, backing up until I'm against the wall. Gina sits down slowly but won't take her eyes off him.

"Where is Mom?" she whispers. "Did she get hurt?"

Mom getting hurt makes sense, but I don't want it to. Gina was worried about Mom walking so far from home in her condition, and she'd argued with Dad. But Mom insisted she'd made it farther before. It's not like she was traveling alone. Dad could come and get help if there was trouble.

Rob half-sits on the edge of the cabinet across from us. He fiddles with his hat in his hands and swallows hard. This is bad; Crazy Rob is never quiet.

"Are we wasting time?" I slide forward and grab a shirt from my side table. "If Mom needs help, we need to get going."

"There's nothing you can do son. They're already gone. Your mom and your dad."

Gone? My body feels cold and my hands start to shake. No. No, that's not possible!

"Where did they take them?" Gina starts to cry. "What happened? The Life First Act says they have to take them to the hospital if they're hurt! They have to save them!"

"Sweetheart ..." Rob steps closer to take her hands. "They were in an autocab on their way home. They were dead as soon as it hit the overpass. There's nothing anybody could have done."

Dead. Nausea rolls over me like a wave I might drown beneath. My eyes start to burn and leak when I squeeze them tight against the pain in my chest.

"That's not possible!" Gina screams. "They can't take an autocab. They have no coin!"

"I saw them myself, Gina," Rob says in a rough voice.

"How? You can't even get that close. If the shields responded, you'd shut down their equipment!"

"I wouldn't tell you if I wasn't sure. You're right, I had to stay back, but Hosni got closer. We used some of my Old World tech to see them through my scope."

Gina's eyes go wide and she grabs Stella Luna's mind-link disk out of her shorts pocket, slipping it behind her right ear. In seconds, the little brown bat flies into my room from the hall, screeching and flitting frantically from one perch to another. God, can her tiny heart take it?

"Gina, what are you doing?" I croak. "You're hurting her!"

Gina ignores me and starts whispering under her breath, "It's okay, Stella. You're safe. Just go see."

"No, Gina, don't look!" Rob shouts.

"Be brave for Momma," she says with a broken voice. "Go see. You know how much we want to go see." She's trying to calm herself so Stella will understand what she wants, but tears are streaming down her face and her hands are shaking.

Stella Luna is part of some kind of old, failed military experiment. When Gina got her from a tech market deal, Stella was already wetwired to the mind-link disk—waiting for a human mind to connect with. A bat's brain and instincts are so different than a human's, though, that Gina can't really control her. They can't talk or reason. Gina can only try to make the bat want to go somewhere, and experience what the little creature senses if it decides to go.

"Listen to me, little girl! It's too horrible!" Rob's voice breaks. "Please, don't look!"

Stella slows down, flits aimlessly around the room for a few more seconds, and leaves through the open window.

"Shit!" Rob leaves the room abruptly.

Nausea hits me again and I look for my bucket to throw up in. I find it by my feet, half under the bed, and bring it up to cradle in my lap. Gina is concentrating now, and I can tell she's trying to navigate Stella to the overpass. Stella never flies straight anywhere so, if it's not close, it takes a lot of concentration to get her to go somewhere specific. I want Stella to get there too, but I wonder if I should rip the mind-link disk off of Gina.

Soon, Yeon-Jae leans her kind, yellow-tan, heavily-wrinkled face around the door frame. Tear tracks are streaked in the layer of dirt on her cheeks. Crazy Rob is close behind her. She comes in and puts her frail arms around Gina from behind. Her lips are moving, so I know she's praying.

Fat lot of good that'll do.

Suddenly, Gina jerks back, nearly knocking over Yeon-Jae and slamming into the wall. Crazy Rob barely catches her as she starts to scream and crumple. My face tingles and my ears start to ring.

She must see them. It must be true … I can't move.

Rob helps her to my bed while Yeon-Jae sits down between us with her hands on us both. Gina curls up on her knees on the foot of the bed, still screaming and holding her head between her hands. The sound is like something out of a nightmare.

"What's happening?" I ask. Then louder, "Can you see them? What's happening?" God, why isn't she saying anything?

"Give her a minute, dear one," Yeon-Jae says to shush me.

Gina starts to scream so hard that her face turns red and her body twists like she's in pain. She claws at the mattress and balls the sheet in her fist. I glance over and Rob is now sitting on the floor in the corner sobbing silently with his hands up over his head, his filthy stocking cap clutched tightly in his fist. I've never seen him like this. Whatever Gina's seeing now, he's seen already.

Yeon-Jae is lying over the top of her now, "I've got you, dear. We're all here with you. Hold on, little one. Old Yeon-Jae's got you. I'm not going to let go."

"What do you see?" I try to shout but my voice is hoarse and unsteady.

Gina hears me this time and her scream turns into a wail. "They're putting them in … in body bags. They're dead."

"How do they know? They need to take them to the hospital!"

"No," she groans.

"They could still be breathing!"

"They aren't."

"How can you be sure? How could Stella—"

"They're not in one piece!" Gina screams, chokes, and starts to cry loudly again.

The bottom falls out of my stomach and even sitting down, I feel like I've somersaulted. I start to cry again too.

"I'm so sorry, beauties," Yeon-Jae says softly, still lying over Gina as she rubs my back. "I'm so sorry."

When our sobbing starts to quiet down, she says, "I know it hurts, but it will be okay. It will take time, but you will be okay … someday … You have to believe."

Oh, what do you know? I bite my tongue against the bitter words, glancing at Mom's unfinished game of chess. Mom and Dad died while I was drawing stupid pictures, crafting a game we'll never play.

My eyes and throat ache, and there is a sharp pain in my chest. My face is soaked with tears. I crawl over to lie down between Gina and the wall, and hold on to my sister as she wails and screams. It feels like we're the only two people left in the world.

No. It's never going to be okay again.

CHAPTER
2

It's been five days.

I stare at the wall of the hell-hole I live in and try not to remember. My stiff joints creak and complain as I draw my blanket tighter around me to keep out the cold breeze that's sweeping through my room from the collapsed corner of the ceiling. God, my joints get worse every fall.

Mom's voice lecturing me about taking care of myself and my home drifts through my mind again, but I can't dredge up the energy to patch it now. At least the breeze takes away the smell of this old mattress.

The agony in my back, neck, and head never let up, and I feel like I weigh 400 pounds instead of about 130. The cannabis is helping me survive my whole world being freakin' annihilated, but it barely touches the pain that keeps me in this bed. The mental games Mom taught me aren't working very well either. Maybe Gina's moonshine would help.

As if summoned by my thoughts, my door creaks open my older sister peeks inside. Her hair is pulled up into a mess on top of her head, and her pale face is streaked with tears. She's got her tech dealer outfit on, so she's been out working again this morning.

Is it still morning?

I want to help, but I'm not well enough to leave home for even an hour or two most days.

"Arthur?" she whispers. "Are you awake?"

"Yeah." I roll over to give her space and she sits down on the edge of my mattress with a sigh.

"Rob says they already, uh ... He says ... they've already been cremated. They've probably thrown out the ashes too."

Shit! "Already?" God, it can't be real. "They didn't even wait to see if anyone would want the ashes?" Community assholes.

"It was obvious they were shirkers." She shrugs. "There's not much we could have done anyway ... I guess."

Our family's been shirkers for generations, and we're even stupid enough to be proud of it. Shirkers are paranoid, and either don't have GRID connections at all or don't use them anymore. Officially, the Global Fellowship labels us the disconnected, but everyone calls us shirkers because we don't contribute our skill or our literal brainpower to the capacity of the system that runs the world. Without a wetware connection, we've got no coin. And apparently, today, being a shirker means we forfeit Mom and Dad's remains to the very assholes they told us to fear. This may be the first time the Global Fellowship has actually succeeded in pissing me off.

I mean, it's really our fault we're miserable. We could join the Community at any time. It's not like anyone's stopping us—me. Well, at least not with Mom and Dad gone.

"They should have tried to find their family!" I grind my teeth as the pain of sitting up shoots through my body. "They were our parents!"

"The Community doesn't think that way." Gina's beautiful two-toned eyes look glassy and hollow.

I know … Goddammit! The Global Fellowship doesn't approve of long-term relationships of any kind. The morons believe they lead to mental anguish, emotional instability, and what used to be called domestic violence in the Old World. These days, Community citizens are raised by the University, not parents. They have no idea who their parents are. That's the biggest way that the Community is wrong.

"If they knew Mom and Dad were shirkers, then they knew they might have a family!" I don't know why I'm arguing with her. She didn't do it.

"It's probably for the best. There wasn't much left anyway." Her voice is so quiet I almost can't hear it.

My argument dies in my throat. I can't think of them that way. I wish we could bury them ... or send them to Dad's home on North Continent.

"Do you think Drustan will come home now?" Gina asks, and seeing the hope in her eyes pisses me off.

Ah yes—Drustan, the great white-knight, and our older half-brother. Never mind that he left us as soon as he was seventeen and hasn't bothered to send word home more than every couple of years since. I was only three, but Gina was six. She looks up to him like some kind of hero.

"Nah." I shake my head. "He's never come before."

"Yeah, but he knew we had Mom and Dad."

"Mom and Dad needed him too, and now they're dead." God, I sound harsh. "It's just us now."

Gina slumps over and stares at her hands. I notice she's developed dark circles beneath her green-brown, starburst eyes.

How can she possibly support us without Dad? I'm sure she hopes Drustan will help, but the ass doesn't care.

"We should still send him a message, so he knows," she whispers.

Now I feel like the ass. "How? Mom and Dad never said how they got letters from him."

"Do you think Joe at Southside knows?"

"Maybe," I lie.

Joe and Drustan were close, but he's run the Southside Brothel nearly since Drustan took off. Drustan hated the Community, so everyone was surprised that Joe joined. It's cool with me. He got a job and I guess with Drustan gone, he didn't want to hang around. I doubt he knows how to get a hold of Drustan anymore, but I decide not to say 'cause I don't wanna break Gina's heart.

I see her wince as she stands up and realize her pain must be high. We were both born with Mom's genetic disease. Gina isn't as bad, but stress makes us worse.

"You okay?" I touch the top of her hand for a second. "You look like you need a nap."

"I wish." She sighs. "I have to go to work, but at least I'll get some booze from Tommy."

"Can you get some for me?"

"I'll try." I'd offer her some cannabis, but she's allergic.

Besides dealing tech in the black market, Gina's voice is amazing. She's got a long-term gig singing at Tommy's bar in District T. We checked Tommy out and the guy's solid. He won't push her into anything she's not comfortable with, and because he's a moonshiner, she can get what she needs to numb the pain a little. It would help if the Community didn't classify everything they consider bad for your health—cannabis, tobacco, alcohol, chems—as illegal. Because of that, we've been a family of criminals all our lives. Being shirkers, we can't get health care or real painkillers.

"Be careful." I sometimes worry some creep will follow her home.

Gina nods and trudges down the hall to the rooms she shared with Mom and Dad. I'm glad I decided to pick out my own place a few years ago. I can't imagine sleeping in there now.

I lean back against the wall, furious that we're so powerless. How's Gina gonna manage? Some days she's almost as disabled as me. Dad's had to support the whole damn family on his own since Drustan left us here to rot. Drustan sure as hell didn't care what was gonna happen to us if he died.

This is so stupid! I rip the blanket off my lap and struggle to my feet. If we were citizens of The Global Fellowship, like the rest of the world, we'd have free food, housing, transportation, medical care, and access to the GRID for life.

I pick up the holoframe beside my bed, watching as the picture of Mom sitting beside the window in their room fades into a picture of Gina and I playing in the street. I'd blame my parents, but it's not their fault. Our family chose the shirker life generations ago because they didn't trust the government. Well, that and we wanted to live as a family.

Gina will try to do it. I know she will. I set the holoframe down and start searching my room for my backpack. She'll work double shifts and worse to pay for both of us to keep living, but her health isn't good enough. She'll kill herself. And for what?

What the hell did I do with … there! I pull the backpack out from under the pile of clothes in the corner and dump out the crap inside.

The Community has every advanced technology that exists. It literally has the resources of the world. No one can make us healthier or our lives better than they can. No one else can give me a way to contribute to the world, instead of merely surviving it. Working server duty is something I could actually do, even with my shitty health.

I'm nineteen. In the Community, I'd have my own hub by now and be supporting myself. I'm not a little kid anymore. Although, it would help if I had gotten around to cleaning more underwear, and where the hell is my good t-shirt?

I'm glad I grew up with my family. I love Gina, but because I love her, I can't be a damn burden on her. She'll never make it if she has to support me. Sure, the Community will sort of run my life, but at least I'll be independent. I'm too sick to have options now anyway. It's the best thing I can do for both of us.

God, I need to stop trembling so hard! I'm only trying to stand for Christ's sake. There's a clinic with a transition center pretty close to here. I can be there in a couple hours.

After my bag is packed, I climb back in bed and lean against it like a pile of pillows. Gina knocks quietly but I pretend to be

asleep, so she leaves without opening the door. She calls for
Stella as they head to Tommy's.

I'm such a jerk to sneak out without saying goodbye … but
she'd stop me.

Fifteen minutes later, I lean on the front door and glance
outside to figure out who's in range. Thank God! Crazy Rob's
nowhere around. Yeon-Jae is asleep in her autorocker with one
of the babies in her lap, poking her face. She's out cold, so no
worry there. The few shrieks from the kids seem pretty far away.
The barrel fires are going strong in their rusty old drums but the
shirkers wandering through them aren't people I recognize.

I hobble out as fast as I can manage without spraining
something. Looking back at the crumbling, graffiti-covered main
door of our building from a safe distance behind an old burned-
out autobus, I breathe a sigh of relief. A chuckle escapes me as I
realize I must look just like Rob.

I swear to you, Gina, I'll come back for you. You'll see. I'll
be okay. I'll be living like a man, and you'll be proud of me.

CHAPTER
3

I'm finally taking control of my own life instead of just letting everything happen to me.

The wind is a steady chill against my neck, and I shiver beneath the overcast sky threatening rain. I've never handled hot or cold very well, and I'm sure as hell not used to being outdoors. Bits of plastic from ages past rustle as they pass me, carried by the breeze from one place to another forever—until someone catches a tiny piece of danger to dispose of it. I really should try but they're moving too fast.

A few kids are playing dodgeball in the street ahead, but the two that I know are absorbed in the game. They're arguing over whether the charger they found will work for the ball when its battery runs down. A couple blocks down, a little girl—maybe six—is begging a woman for something to eat, but the woman isn't answering. She looks like she might be a heavy stunner, but it could be chems. I wish I had something to give the kid.

I decide to go to the clinic in District S because Tommy's is in District T. If Gina or Stella see me while I'm still struggling to get there, we'll just end up in a fight.

As I hobble my way down the old cracked and pitted, textured-glass streets, I try to distract myself from the pinch and throb of each step. I can't believe I'm actually escaping the Dregs, one of the largest God-forsaken shirker camps in Central Continent. Mom says this ancient city was prosperous centuries ago—before the wars—because it sat at the intersection of trade routes and major rivers. Now it sits abandoned between Sectors 10 and 11.

We use the crumbling buildings like homes, and there are enough options for most people to pick their own room for a burrow. Around the barrel fires, people here tell stories about the old shipping containers or abandoned mining tunnels they've lived in. It used to make me thankful we had it so good—before I understood how freakin' well Community citizens live.

Once again, I remember Yeon-Jae's tanned, amazingly-wrinkled face. Every time I was more than fed up with the misery of this place, she'd shush me, look me in the eyes and say, "Remember you're lucky, Arthur. Many people in this world have a place to stay. Very few have homes." She's as crazy as Rob.

Even though most shirkers are wanderers, my family has called the Dregs home for as long as I can remember. Dad spent his life telling the shirkers here all about a God the world stopped believing in centuries ago. A lot of good that did.

Now I look up at the ruined building Gina was trying to convince Mom and Dad to move into. I can tell it's the one because it still has an old tower at the top. God, it makes me sick to think she actually wants to live there. It's at least ten stories taller than the other buildings, but the middle floors look like they might be open to bad weather. Gina was telling us there's a local guy who thinks one of the first-floor bathrooms is still connected to the District S water and sewer system. He told her he might be able to get it working. Even as close as it is to Community housing, here on the border of the district, the Community won't let something like that slide.

Everything will be different now though. This new life will be all I've ever wanted—running water, fresh-cooked meals, and most of all something to help this constant agony. I've heard that even the most basic Community hubs have a sink with running water, a real freakin' toilet, and a shower. After I'm set up, I'll get Gina to sneak in and try it out—even she won't be able to turn down a hot shower. I'm finally going to enjoy everything the Community has to offer, and I'll be carrying my own weight.

Ha! That's stupidly ironic when I can barely shoulder this backpack. I should have left my crap at home to retrieve later, but I wanted a clean break.

The crosswalk beneath me bridges the Dregs and civilization. Real excitement builds in my gut, even over the pain. I've been here before, but it's shocking to see the sudden change from ruin and putrid filth to clean well-maintained streets and buildings. It's like someone drew an imaginary line across the landscape, almost like in fiction books, that when you cross you enter another world. The crosswalk is illuminated inside the road glass. The little lights activate in front of me, one foot at a time, until I've crossed the road safely.

I'll come back for Gina when I can show her that she doesn't need to take care of me anymore. Without me, she'll be able to support herself; she won't need Prince Drustan to save her either.

The bone-deep ache in my legs, back, and shoulders escalates steadily to a shrill pitch, but I can't stop to rest. If I do, I'll lose my momentum, stiffen up, and won't be able to get started again. I focus on turning the pain into white noise, and the effort keeps me from worrying or second-guessing. I've walked so far now; I'd never make it back if I turned around.

Just a few more blocks.

After what seems like hours, relief washes over me as I catch sight of the clinic. The sun glints off the tall, blocky building's shiny marble exterior. There are curved metal benches outside, and a couple of small patches of pristine, green grass. It all looks so perfect.

Shit. My brief flare of hope breaks my focus and doubles my awareness of the pain.

When I reach the front door, it opens automatically, and as I enter, a warm wall of air welcomes my wind-bitten cheeks— God, I hate the fall. I don't have a Citizen's ID or CID yet for the building to register when I walk in, so I know I'm immediately flagged as a shirker. I'll get one when my brain is wetwired and registered. After that, I'll be able to access the GRID and function as a server for several hours a day to earn coin.

The waiting area has a couple of dozen mauve chairs lined up in neat rows, with a single door to ADMITTING and several self-service kiosks along the wall. Most of the people in here are wearing the same clothes—jeans and white t-shirts. Many of them are staring at me. I guess I look dirty. Do I smell? I wish I'd found that cleaner shirt. I try to ignore them as I head for a kiosk.

GOOD AFTERNOON, it chirps in a cheery voice. WHAT ARE YOUR NEEDS TODAY? I quickly touch the box for

PRIVATE MODE. I don't need everybody listening in on my crap.

I select JOIN/REJOIN THE GLOBAL FELLOWSHIP on the touchscreen, thankful that I don't have to answer out loud. I guess it's probably obvious though. I enter my name, ARTHUR COMYN MALLOREY. NO, I haven't been a Community member before. NO, I'm not signing anyone else up for citizenship. NO, I haven't been inoculated before. NO, I don't have a place to live. Gina would freak out if my answers led someone home.

The kiosk asks, DO YOU WANT TO PARTICIPATE IN A FREE HEALTH SCREENING?

I stare at the screen until my eyes begin to burn. My heart races, which is dumb because this is the whole reason I'm here. Mom was terrified of being identified as ill or disabled. She'd act like we'd be locked up in an institution. Hell, even if I do end up in one, it's got to be better than the Dregs. At least I'd have a clean place to sleep.

I close my eyes, draw air deep into my lungs, and hold my breath while I answer: YES, I want a health screening. I let my breath out slowly and feel a disorienting mixture of excitement and finality.

An armrest slides out of the wall. PLEASE PLACE YOUR ARM PALM-UP AS INDICATED ON SCREEN. When I do, a thin band descends to clip around my forearm and take my blood pressure, oxygen saturation, and pulse. Then the kiosk scans my skin and draws a finger-sized vial of blood.

CONGRATULATIONS! It startles me when the armrest is jerked back out of sight and silent fireworks display on the screen. HAVE A SEAT. A TRANSITION COORDINATOR WILL BE WITH YOU SHORTLY.

I limp over to the padded, mauve chair closest to the admitting door, drop my pack, and collapse. My spine is now throbbing, my right hip is out of place, and I'm so exhausted I can't stop trembling. I close my eyes to focus on tuning out the pain.

CHAPTER
4

"Arthur Mallorey," a smooth female voice booms from overhead.

The admitting door opens just as my eyes do and a man in purple scrubs walks toward me. My body has been stiffening as I sit and when I stand up to meet him, I clench my teeth to hold back a cry of pain. I keep my eyes open, steadying myself against the side of the chair. Hopefully, I look like I'm trying to remember something, instead of waiting for my vision to clear.

"Arthur? Go ahead and leave that here," the man says. He has coppery skin, chestnut brown hair, and a high tenor voice.

No way am I going to leave this lying around. Every shirker knows, if you leave it for a minute, you're giving it away. Before I can grab my backpack though, the man picks it up and slings it over his shoulder. He slumps only minutely under the weight of my life.

"That's my—"

"It's no problem." He heads straight to the door. "I'm Dr. Ervine. Normally you'd be attended by a Transition Coordinator through your welcoming, Arthur, but I took a look at your health screening. The Coordinator will collect your belongings from the examination room. Follow me."

Okay ... I resist the urge to ask why my health screening changes things. As the admitting door shuts behind us, a nervous tremor races through my stomach—don't be an idiot. There's no reason to be paranoid.

"You have a very serious genetic abnormality," the doctor says.

Yeah, no kidding.

After rounding a couple of corners, we enter a tiny room. There's just enough space for him to navigate around the examination table and access its steel drawers and cabinets. The walls are a light yellow color and the floor is simple white tile. Everything in here looks crazy clean.

"We rarely see cases of Ehlers-Danlos Syndrome anymore. I expect you're in need of immediate medical care, so we're going to skip a few steps."

Sweet! Who knew that being sick would be a fast pass to getting through this place?

"Sure." I shrug, trying to sound casual. I ignore the pinch in my neck that prevents my right shoulder from lifting quite as high as my left.

"How would you rate your pain now, on a scale of one to ten, with one being barely noticeable and ten being the worst you can imagine?" He sets my backpack on the floor by the door and motions for me to sit on the examination table.

"Uh, like a six I guess." The worst pain I can imagine makes me blackout. I shrug again and a twinge makes me wince—stupid neck! I rub my right hand against my left forearm to try and steady their shaking.

"Let's try some of this, shall we?" He fills a syringe with something clear.

"What is it?" I lean away.

"It's a medication that targets your sodium channels and nervous system for long-term pain reduction. I've combined it with a fast-acting anesthetic. It's completely safe, and should provide you some immediate relief."

I hold out my arm and accept the shot. After a brief burning sensation, a blessed numbness washes through me. The relief is such a sharp sensation that it's almost a secondary pain—thank you, God. Tears immediately flood my eyes and I start to topple.

"Careful now." Dr. Ervine grabs my arm and holds me upright. Back and arm supports begin to rise out of the examination table.

"I'm sorry." I choke on my tears. Jeez, this is embarrassing.

"It's alright." He smiles, raising leg supports to help me recline. "Resisting constant pain requires a lot of strength. Sometimes when a patient's pain is removed, their strength goes with it for a moment. Now, I need to talk to you about your future care. How well do you understand your condition?"

"Well, I've lived with it for almost twenty years." I chuckle and wipe away the tears. "I think I get the gist of it by now. Mom had it too."

No matter how good I feel, I can't ever tell anyone about Gina. She doesn't want an official record that she exists. I wonder if he learned about Ehlers-Danlos in school, or if he got the information from the GRID? We just call it EDS.

"Well, it's my ethical obligation to make sure you understand it fully," Dr. Ervine says. "We can't rely on non-expert explanations for our health decisions. You have a variant of a genetic disorder called Ehlers-Danlos Syndrome that makes many of your connective tissues—like skin, ligaments, and tendons—weak and stretchy, and your joints hypermobile.

"Essentially, your DNA carries a bad blueprint, so to speak, for collagen. Collagen is the fibrous protein that gives your cells their strength or their rigidity. When it's mismade, it causes your tissues to be fragile, slow to heal, and sometimes dysfunctional. It can also affect the endocrine system—your hormones. Which of your systems are affected depends on the specific genetic mutations you inherited as well as how your body uniquely expresses those mutations."

"Yeah, I know that." Without all the fancy words.

"Very good."

He blinks a couple of times and gets that glassy-eyed look people have when they're reading information the GRID is sending directly into their brain—man, that must be cool. I close my eyes to rest until he starts talking again.

"It looks like the mutations you present are pretty standard, but there are a couple of issues we need to watch," he says, finally focusing back on me. "It looks like you probably know about the easy bruising already, and I'm assuming you know your joints can sublux, dislocate and injure easily?"

"Yeah." The pain is gone but it's still hard to move my head. "I dislocate things a lot. My knees, hips, shoulders, elbows, and some of my fingers. My mom used to have us use braces when we could find them, but they didn't always work." The corner of my mouth lifts when I think of how often people call my chronic sickness falling apart.

"It's not just dislocations," Dr. Ervine sighs. "Hypermobility means the range of motion of your joints is too wide. Patients with your condition tend to develop bad habits and postures trying to compensate for joints that bend much too far even without dislocating. Those habits can lead to further laxity and injury, and an early onset of arthritic symptoms. Custom-fitted braces for each problem area are essential, and we should begin administering regular injections to tighten things up and prevent further injury as much as possible."

"Okay." Regular injections? Well, if it helps, I guess.

"Now, I need to run a quick scan for the most urgent complications." He blinks a couple of times and a long, black tube descends from an opening in the ceiling. It moves about like a snake as it heads for my chest.

"Whoa, what the hell is that?" I start to try to get off the table, but he holds down on my shoulder.

"It's nothing to be afraid of. It's just a scanner. Stay very still for a few moments. I need to take some quick imaging of your heart and abdominal cavity."

"Why?" I ask, watching it closely.

It stops about six inches from my chest and starts making a faint whirring sound, emitting a band of blue light. After it travels up and down the whole surface of my torso, he closes his eyes and goes quiet again.

"Good. There isn't any aortic dilation," the doctor says without opening his eyes. "Ah, but yes, genes don't lie. Arthur, do you experience regular nausea and constipation?"

Oh, yikes. Can't they just fix that without talking to me about it? "Yeah. So? I throw up like every other day, but in between, I'm good."

"No, you're not." He opens his eyes and looks at me again as the scanning tube withdraws into the ceiling. "The nausea may fade, but your genes are also affecting your intestines."

"What? How?"

He points to a mirror on the wall that suddenly changes to display what looks like a 3-D scan of my insides. Gross.

"Intestines are made up of strong muscles that move food along through the digestive system as the body absorbs nutrients," he says. "Unfortunately in your case, those muscles and tissues are weak. Instead of pushing the food along, they stretch and bulk up, resulting in multiple chronic blockages. This kind of buildup in your system will make absorbing nutrition difficult at best, but at its worst can actually poison you.

"I'm going to give you some medication to take after you get back to your assigned housing. Don't take it until you can rest for at least twelve hours. You'll be given the medication when you leave for the day."

"Okay." Jeez, doesn't that sound like fun?

Dr. Ervine's fingers twitch as he must be interacting with my GRID record. "Now, were you raised by your birth mother?"

The reminder is like a punch to the gut. I swallow a few times before I can answer. "By both my parents. They ... they died a few nights ago." My eyes start to burn, and my voice sounds rough.

The doctor looks up with a serious expression. "Are you experiencing any depression?"

"Well, yeah."

The doctor nods and digs through a cabinet on the wall. "My apologies. I had assumed your depleted levels of serotonin were due to chronic pain. We're going to start you on a low-dose antidepressant."

We are?

He walks over and administers another shot of medicine. I just watch him. I'm sure he knows what's best better than I do.

"Unfortunately, long-term relationships can lead to Obsessive Attachment Syndrome, or OAS, and very serious health complications after events like this. Can you read? I noticed you were able to interact with the admitting kiosk after deactivating the auditory instructions."

"Yes." I resent the assumption that shirkers are ignorant, even though I know in the Dregs it's often true. Mom made sure we could read, write, and do pretty complex math.

"Excellent. I'll provide patient informational records on OAS for your review later. You will likely require counseling, but at least now, separation from them will enable you to begin healing."

Screw you, asshole! You have no idea what you're talking about! He actually thinks Mom and Dad dying was good for me instead of screwing over my whole freakin' life! I clench my fist until it throbs to keep from punching the guy in the jaw, but I'd better not reinforce their idiotic beliefs that love and family lead to violence. I try to breathe deeply and slowly as he silently twitches his fingers for a few moments.

"You'll be assigned temporary housing during your placement process," he resumes without looking up. "There you will have GRID access through manual interfaces until you're moved into permanent housing. The wetware connections in your brain will grow in the interim. Has anyone explained the inoculation process to you?"

I understand it at a very basic level because of the tech that Gina deals in. I may as well hear the full rundown, though, if I'm actually going to let them do it. "Sorta, but not really."

He opens a drawer and pulls out an injector that looks vaguely like a miniaturized version of Dad's antique caulking gun. I stiffen. The end they stick against your skin is almost an inch wide! How many injectors are in that space?

"This is what we use to administer the inoculation. The injection includes all the basic vaccines you should have been given when you were two, and the components required to grow your GRID connection. Your natural bioelectric current will facilitate the growth of structures based on buckyballs and nanotubes, from carbon already existing inside your body. Those structures will form the necessary organic connections your brain needs to communicate with the GRID. Absolutely no inorganic hardware will be installed inside your body. The injection may cause a mild-to-severe headache, but the process is completely internal and completely safe."

I swallow around the lump in my throat. No wonder they do it to little kids right after they get them from their birth mothers. They don't have to understand what's going on and won't remember it. Oh well. It's not like I can go back in time.

"I'm ready." I nod, willing it to be true.

"Then, I have some documentation for you." He pulls a flex and a scrawl out of his drawer. The thin, flexible piece of smart glass displays some kind of standard waiver form.

Good God. There's at least 50 pages of fine print here! I'd have to sit in this room for hours to read it all.

Screw that. I scroll through the pages quickly, only glancing over the important bits, and use the scrawl to sign my name to all the highlighted boxes. Then I hand them both back and brace for the next step.

"Go ahead and relax. I'll get everything ready." He loads a scary-huge vial of shimmery, green liquid into the injector, and circles around to stand behind me as a section of the backrest disappears from the space behind my neck. I feel the cool bite of an alcohol swab against the back of my neck only briefly, and then pressure as the injector is applied. "Here we go."

There is a sharp pain and burning sensation, followed by an incredible sense of pressure building at the base of my skull.

"OW, Jesus!" I ball my hands into fists and resist the urge to pull away until he finishes. Sure enough, a mild headache starts building immediately.

The doctor comes around and looks at me with raised eyebrows. "Are you religious?"

No way am I going to tell him my family is Christian. That would put me into the lunatic category forever as far as these people are concerned. Gina's no preacher like Dad, but she's pretty hard-core. It's never really been my thing.

"No. It's just an expression ... That hurt." I rub at the mild pain in the back of my neck.

The doctor sighs and nods. "The headache will linger for the next several days, but the pain medication should help with that. Your daily medications will be delivered to your temporary housing—then to your permanent arrangement of course.

"Now, given your condition, I'm going to run you through a series of full skeletal and soft-tissue imaging studies to assess what damage you've already accumulated. It'll help us determine what care you require. Afterward, check out at the kiosk you used when you arrived. You'll receive clothing and hygiene rations, and directions to your housing unit. Do you have any questions?"

"I don't think so." I'll probably have a million as I go along, but I'll ask then.

A woman with blond hair and light green scrubs opens the examination room door and steps inside.

"Good," the doctor says, giving me a firm handshake. I'm surprised that it doesn't hurt my hand. He motions to the new woman. "This is Desiree. She'll escort you to our imaging level."

Man, my pain is better, but I'm exhausted. "Can I come back and do it tomorrow?"

"It's best to get it done now. Follow Desiree."

Great ... Well, I'm going to be a wreck tomorrow anyway.

CHAPTER
5

I place my thumb on the little glass panel and the door to my new hub pops open. There's a wide hallway leading into the main room with a bathroom in the space to my left. The right side of the hallway has a closet with a short rod for hanging clothes and a few built-in drawers. It looks like it's already stocked with the clothing rations they sent over from the clinic.

Wow. This is totally freakin' awesome! I want to explore, but it takes all my strength to struggle over and collapse on the full-sized bed instead.

Crap! I forgot to shut the door. I start pushing myself up on trembling arms when I hear a hiss from behind me. The door is closing itself? Okay. That's freaky.

"You have to be careful with your safety, Arthur," a woman's voice says.

I freeze. "Who ... who's there?"

I look around the room wildly but don't see anyone. A skinny table and a rolling chair are to the right of the bed, and a nightstand with a single drawer and cabinet door is on the other side. At the foot, there's a huge mirror. The far corner of the room is a kitchen with a mini-fridge, sink, and small cooking station not much wider than me. Before my eyes can sweep back around to the other side, an image starts to shimmer beside me on the bed. I gasp and roll away from the woman now sitting there.

"My name is Manuela," she says with a smile, "but I can change it to whatever you would prefer."

"Oh, I've heard of you!"

I've never seen her before though. She has bronzed skin, black hair with blond highlights, and rich brown eyes. She's wearing what looks exactly like the clothing rations I was given—a white t-shirt and jeans. It looks much better on her than it looks on me. Wait. How am I seeing this without a wetware connection?

"How the hell am I seeing you?" I glance around but don't see anything obvious.

"This housing unit was built for transitioning citizens. The Global Fellowship does not wish for you to be deprived of the services the GRID can offer while you wait for your connection to grow. Therefore, everything in this room is customized to allow you manual interaction with my systems."

"Yeah, but how am I seeing you?"

"There are sixty microprojectors built into each room that allow me to project a physical presence. Would you like to customize my name or appearance?"

"Why?"

"I will be your life companion. I am the AI that assists every Community member with their daily needs. It is appropriate for my appearance to be as pleasing as possible. I am fully customizable."

"I'm too tired," I say, rolling onto my back.

"I can see that. You must take care of yourself, Arthur. I can complete some basic tasks like opening and closing your door or ordering items you need. However, I am limited in my physical ability. What you see is merely a projection."

"Yeah, sorry about the door. Mom used to get on my case about that too."

"You knew your mother?"

I examine the texture on the ceiling for a minute or two.

"I'm sorry. Have I said something that has upset you?"

"You can tell?" I shove a pillow under my head, trying to get more comfortable.

"I interact with millions of citizens every year," she says with a slight frown. "I have learned to read body language nearly as well as a human."

"I guess I'm kinda homesick." I wish Gina was here. It's going to be harder than I thought to go a few weeks without seeing her. "Mom and Dad died a few days ago."

"Both of them?" She looks surprised.

"Yeah, an autocab accident." Wait a sec. My heart starts to beat hard enough I can feel it in my ears. "Are you the one who runs those things?" I don't know enough about the AI that manage everything.

"They are operated by the GRID ... but no, not by me. I submit requests and destinations, but all automated vehicles are run through a transportation management AI."

"Oh." Relief washes over me and makes me a little dizzy. Thank God I'm lying down.

"I believe I heard about the accident in question. Did this happen near the encampment of the disconnected between Sectors 10 and 11?"

"Yeah." I roll over onto my side and curl up, trying to find a position that will relieve the tension in my muscles. Just talking about it makes the pain start to cut back through the medication.

Manuela extends a projected hand and rests it on my own. I don't feel it, but I get it. "How are you feeling about their passing?"

"You're programmed to ask how I feel?" It's almost funny.

"Correct. In addition to assisting you with daily tasks, I am fully programmed to monitor your physical and mental health needs. Many important symptoms and concerns arise during daily life that a citizen may not remember to report to their physicians. I am also equipped with strategies and suggestions to improve your condition."

"Really? Like what?"

"You have spent all day processing through the health clinic, correct? I have observed that you are very weary. Would you like for me to run a hot shower for you?"

Oh, man. "A hot shower sounds great, but I can't stand up that long." Should I admit I've never had one before?

"No need," Manuela says with a chuckle. Odd, coming from a computer. "The doctors knew the extent of your physical needs when they recommended this room for you." A small door in the corner of the room slides open and a motorized wheelchair comes driving up to the bed. "If you would like to take off your clothes, I can escort you into the shower. There is both a personal lift and a chair built in for you."

Whoa, cool. But it's weird to undress with a woman watching. Should I make her male? No, that would be even weirder. I start to struggle out of my clothes.

"Is it difficult to talk about your feelings with an AI? I can schedule you an appointment with a counselor."

"No!" I hold a hand up and nearly topple on my face with my shirt tangled around my arm. "No, I'm okay. I don't need any of that stuff. I just... it hurts, but I'll be fine."

"What were your parents' names?"

"Uh, Mom was Lynneth, Lynneth Mallorey. And my dad was … Rory. They've already been cremated because we're shirkers. … God, I wish I could have seen them again." My voice cracks at the admission and I toss my shirt to the floor.

"Do you believe access to their remains would assist you in finding closure and moving on?"

"Absolutely!" I bolt upright, my heart racing. "Why?"

"The records indicate that your parents' remains have not been disposed of yet."

"Can I have them? Like in an urn or something?" Gina would love that!

"It is not part of my core programming," she says with a shrug, "but I have observed this form of grief in hundreds of thousands of citizens. Humans seem to improve when provided the chance to dispose of the remains on their own."

"Oh my God, that would be amazing!"

Manuela smiles. "See? Your spirits are improving already. The doctors would advise you that disposing of the remains in a way that affords you closure should be done as soon as possible, to promote healing and separation."

That's weird. "Do you believe that crap?"

She looks thoughtful for a moment. "I would say that my observations are inconsistent and inconclusive. However, the advisement is standard protocol. You should not keep the remains in your possession for any significant duration."

"Sure thing." I nod with a smile, wiping away a few tears. "I swear. I'll put Mom and Dad's ashes somewhere they would have wanted right away." I'll get them to Gina.

"Alright then, I will have the remains shipped here. The shower is ready when you are, Arthur."

"Oh, yeah. Right." Tossing away the rest of my clothes, I slide down onto the waterproof padding of the wheelchair.

Manuela offers to put me in the shower with the lift but I'm not that bad off yet, though I tremble a bit as I climb onto the shower seat. The hot water is glorious!

"Thanks," I say. "It's nice not to be alone."

"You're welcome," she says with a warm smile. "Next, we will find out what kind of things you enjoy. You have a lot of life to fit into the coming weeks."

CHAPTER
6

"Arthur, how high is your pain today?" Manuela asks as light skitters across my closed eyelids.

"I'm fine." I sigh. "It's only like a one or a two."

"Is it still the inoculation headache?"

"Yeah, mostly."

"You haven't been out of bed all day."

Because that medicine they gave me made me spend half a week in the bathroom praying not to die! "This is normal, Manni. I have to do this a lot." Hell, she's as bad as Gina— always worrying about something. The reminder turns my stomach.

"It's important to build up your strength and endurance during periods when you can be more active." After a few minutes of silence, she asks, "Is there something that has upset you?"

Yes, but nothing I am going to tell the mother of all computers. That would be the ultimate betrayal. "No. I told you, I'm fine."

Remembering Gina's face yesterday, I burrow deeper under the blankets. She was on her way home from Tommy's. I thought it would be harmless enough to ride the autobus along her normal route to see if I could catch sight of her and see how she was doing—she looked terrible. She was showing people on the street my picture and asking the shirkers if they'd seen me. She had Stella searching too. For a moment I'd thought that stupid bat had caught sight of me, but she was after a bug.

God, I never meant to hurt Gina that much. I need to get back to her soon and let her know I'm okay. But she thinks like Mom. If she knew where I am, she'd be terrified. No, I can't tell her until I can show her I'm really going to take care of us.

"Manni, how long before the wetware connection is finished growing?"

"It varies from person to person, but they won't check your connection for another week."

"A week? Dammit." Gina's going to kill me.

"Is there something you need your connection for? I can facilitate any transaction for you."

"Like what?" I roll over and look at her. "I've got nothing to spend."

"Yes, you do." She rolls her eyes. "You were given 10,000 GRIDcoin when you signed up for citizenship. You will receive 5,000 more for each of the Community integration assessments you complete. The ones I told you about on Monday."

"What?" I need to pay better attention. "What can I get?"

"Not much. Perhaps a couple of small items. Oh, and I have been notified that your parents' remains will arrive today."

"Whoa, what?" I sit up and feel instantly dizzy. "When?"

"Be careful not to fall, Arthur," she says, looking concerned. "I reminded you last time that I have no way to pick you up without sending for medical assistance."

"Don't you dare call them if I fall. Well, unless I say so. Or… or if I'm bleeding, I guess. I told you, it'll pass, and I'll get up."

"I am responsible for your welfare." Her projection sits cross-legged on the bed beside me.

"How much do you know about gimps like me? How we feel?"

"I've cared for very few ambulatory invalids, but I do have access to research and other information on the subject."

I wince at the term but it's probably accurate. "Yeah, well you should know I won't appreciate you calling people for help every time I have a minor crisis. We invalids find that pretty freakin' upsetting."

"Your physical welfare and security are my first priorities."

"Well, I guarantee you, Manni. Stress like that will make my pain spike up and tank my freakin' physical welfare."

"Thank the sciences I'm not human." She sighs. "You have so many delicate systems."

"You were created by humans."

Manuela shrugs. "As to your previous question, the ashes will be arriving at 3 o'clock by drone. They will be left on your balcony. Your new braces should arrive in the same shipment."

"I already have braces," I say, as I lean back against the headboard.

"The doctors determined based on your medical scans that your current equipment is ill-fitting and too worn for proper function. They've had custom braces designed and printed for each joint that needs stabilization or alignment correction. You will also receive new shoes with custom-printed insoles to correct for the hypermobility in your feet. They believe your impaired gait is increasing the instability in your upper body."

"Wow, that's cool." I wonder if Gina would do better if she had braces that fit right. "Can anybody order braces like that?"

"Any citizen can, but it has to be ordered through their medical team."

Damn. There goes that idea. "What will Mom and Dad's ashes be in?"

"Their ashes will be in biodegradable bags in a standard recycled aluminum shipping box."

"Do I have enough to buy an urn? ... Do they even make them?"

"Yes, urns are still manufactured. I will see if any are available locally."

The reflective surface of the giant mirror across from my bed disappears as it switches to display mode, and Manuela brings up the commissary. She's navigating too quickly for me to follow, but eventually, the screen pauses with options displayed.

"Three options are available for use in immediate services. Again, the Community recommends citizens not hold onto items of attachment for long periods. Both the golden and olive options are designed for the remains of a single individual, so they will likely be too small to hold both remains. However, this teal option should be sufficient. It would cost 7,000 GRIDcoin."

Yikes. That's almost everything I have. ... Nothing else is more important though.

"That will work." I nod. "Then I can carry them with some dignity."

"Shall I place the purchase?"

"Yeah, go ahead." Manni completes the transaction and the screen says the urn will be delivered tomorrow morning. "What other stuff do they have?"

"Almost anything you can dream of, excluding military supplies." She brings up and points to a huge list of categories.

"Do they have art stuff?" I ask, remembering my easel and unfinished monster back home. I couldn't bear to bring it, but something new might pass the time. Maybe I could make Gina a card and find a way to get it to her without letting on where I am. If I do it right, she'll stop worrying. Oh man, that would be great!

"I have access to over 10,000 options for artistic expression. Are you an artist, Arthur?"

"Not really, but I like to draw. Game characters mainly."

"Please define game characters."

"You know, for role-playing games."

"There are many RPGs on the GRID. Which do you play?"

"Oh, no. Not GRIDgames. The Old World kind, where people get together to make up characters and stories—like D&D."

"Do people still play those, Arthur?" she asks, looking surprised. "I only have historical records of such games."

"We used to." Suddenly, all I can hear is Gina screaming. My eyes are burning and there is a sharp pain in the middle of my chest that makes it difficult to breathe.

"Who used to play with you, Arthur?"

I'm not going to answer that by crying and prove to her that I have OAS. Instead, I lie back down and curl up in a ball with the blanket over my head. I'd better stay away from drawing for a while too, or Manni might have all kinds of symptoms to report to my doctors. I can't handle them trying to cure me right now without losing my mind.

"Are you sad?"

God, that stupid question is even worse. Of course I'm sad. I've lost my whole damn family. Anyone with a human heart would know why. They'd expect it. ... Well, Dr. Ervine the Asshole didn't but that was because of his stupid Community education. Hell, in the Community, friendship, love, family or anything like real community is seen as a disease. I snort at how ridiculously ironic it is.

"You can also order entertainment of several varieties."

Manni's obviously changing the subject, so I decide to pretend it's working. "Like books?"

"If you would like to read books, I can request them through the global digital library at no cost. Visual and auditory programs are similar. However, you would need to purchase escorts or sexual services."

"Sexual services?" Man, did I just squeak? That's just great. I'm never coming out from under this blanket again.

"Yes. Your options are displayed on the mirror."

I'm almost afraid to look. Then again, I will eventually. Right? I fold down the blanket just enough to see a huge list of names and faces scrolling by. "Whoa, wait. Are the people from Southside on there?"

"There are 32 women, 30 men, and 27 transgendered individuals listed from the Sector 10, District S Brothel."

"Is Joe still the manager there?" I dry my eyes and sit back up to see better.

"There is a Joe Strauss listed as manager. Here is his photo, but he does not offer sexual services."

Oh, ick. "Yeah, I wouldn't expect him to." I snicker. "He's not really the type."

"Would you like me to place an order for you? You do not have enough GRIDcoin for in-person services, but you could afford services for your view screen."

"Uh, no. Thanks." I wipe my hands over my face. "I'm … still a mess right now."

"Very well. Would you like me to bring up a physical therapy tutorial?"

"Do you have anything for someone like me?"

"The therapy library contains every injury and condition that is known, including the symptoms of Ehlers-Danlos Syndrome. Your medical team has flagged the most relevant exercises for the complications you experience."

"Well, I should start getting myself in better shape then, huh?"

"That is a healthy decision, Arthur. You should be proud."

Yeah, sure. I'll get right on that.

Okay, I've got a plan now—at least. I hate to, but I'd better wait to see Gina until I'm working server duty and making steady coin or she'll freak. For now, I'll get Mom and Dad's ashes to her. Gina sells tech in Joe's black market meets so he can get it to her easy. I'll explain later.

When I go home, I'll have to use CID jammers, but I can get them from Joe too. I'll show her how much coin I make, and we'll figure out how to split it. I won't need it all. She won't have medical care, but she could use it to buy chems on the black market. She'll be able to rest and take care of herself more.

This is great!

CHAPTER
7

I walk into Southside Brothel feeling like a trillion coin. I've got braces for my back, knees, ankles, and wrists. The physical therapy is really starting to help, the medicine is keeping my pain down, and my headache disappeared a couple of days ago.

My new hub is absolutely perfect with Manuela there to help. I'm wearing clean clothes, and it's awesome to have a haircut and clean shave. I can take a shower every day!

I went ahead and breezed through the assessments she told me about. With some coin finally in my account, I decided it's time to see Joe. One of the working women touches me casually as I walk past—God, it's embarrassing to blush so easy.

Joe is standing behind the front counter arguing with an angry chick who's dressed like a tech dealer. Whoa … Gina would kill for a pair of pants like that! They've got at least a dozen pockets on each side for stashing tech—probably shielded too. Her weirdly-long legs provide a lot of room for pockets. Even Gina's aren't that long. The chick's a little out of proportion, but somehow it makes her exotically pretty.

Because of Gina I know, besides his official gig managing the brothel, Joe coordinates the black market in this sector. Some deal must be going sideways. His bright blue eyes are intense, and the right one is twitching like it always does when he's upset. When I reach them, I nod to get his attention but he's too focused on the angry chick.

"Look, I'm sorry," Joe is saying, "but I don't make the rules. You know better than anyone. I have to do what they—"

"That's bullshit!" the woman shouts, slamming her palm down on the counter. "I deserve the same service as everyone else!"

Are those feathers in her blond hair? I would swear they are. I lean in, trying to see. There are only a few of them, but they're long and so shaggy-looking that they blend in with the hair strands.

Wait a minute ... What are they arguing about?

"I know you do, Selena," Joe pleads, "and I feel like shit, but I can't risk—"

Without warning, Selena reaches over the counter, grabs Joe by the front of his shirt, and lifts him clear off the ground. Whoa! Joe is like six-foot-two. He's not quite as tall as me, but he's heavier.

Bringing back her other fist to punch him in the face, she shouts, "Don't mess with me, you lousy sack of—"

"Hey, wait!" I put a hand on her shoulder.

In a split second, her head pivots around completely backward and she's hissing in my face. Holy shit! She's a freakin' chimera!

I stumble back and land on my ass. Somehow, I keep the box in my hands from spilling. She drops Joe back behind the counter and now my brain finally kicks in with how the hell she's so strong. I've heard of chimeras all my life, but I've never seen one before.

Chimeras are genetic leftovers from the Old World supersoldier programs in the early part of this millennium. Much of the world was in either a hot or cold war, and it was the dawn of the genetic age. Scientists knew just enough to be incredibly dangerous, and naturally, most governments started experimenting with lacing animal DNA into the human genome to produce desired traits—enhanced senses, strength, speed, agility, and natural weaponry.

Most of the chimeras were so malformed they didn't survive, but there were significant successes. Once the public found out, the experiments were banned but they didn't really stop for decades. Now sometimes, those genetics pop back up. Pandora's box was not just open, but actively breeding with the human population.

A shudder of fear runs down my spine, but my brain is still trying to work out the puzzle—which is stupid. Chimeras don't have the traits of only one order or class of animals.

She hisses again, keeping her eyes on me as the rest of her body spins my direction. She crouches down to look me in the eye. "You got a problem, little boy?"

Then it hits me. An owl! Wow, I've never even heard of a chimera with owl genetics before! Her face is heart-shaped and unusually flat. She has a very thin, very small nose resting low between eyes twice the size they should be. She has incredibly faint, white feathers running above her brow and along her cheeks, but they're so small they look almost like fur. Her ears look a little off-kilter too—like somehow one is higher than the other.

"Staring at the chimera, are you?" she sneers.

"No." I try to swallow the lump in my throat. "But your feathers are real pretty." What the hell did I just say? Backtrack, Stupid! "And my sister would kill for those pants."

The beautiful, terrifying chimera cocks her head to one side and examines me for a moment. Then she snorts. "You've never seen someone like me before." She traces a wicked-sharp fingernail very lightly across my cheek.

"No," I admit, "but I don't get out much."

After a moment, she laughs. I mean, really, truly laughs so hard she holds her sides. It's a girly sound to come from such a badass chick. Then something seems to sober her and her face wilts into a frown. She looks back at me and holds my chin in her hand the way Mom used to do. It makes my chest ache.

"Tell you what, kid." She sighs. "They don't serve my kind here anymore, but you'd better get a little more experience under your belt while you still can. You seem like you deserve better."

God, I've got to stop blushing!

She helps me to my feet, and I try really hard not to think about how easily she could kill me. Then she notices the box in my arms.

"Who's in there?" She can tell that it's human remains? "Don't ask, kid. I just know."

"Uh, my parents."

"Parents? Plural?"

"Yeah. Lived, loved, and died together and all that. Now all I have is a box."

"You're lucky," she says, obviously looking down at my braces. "Don't forget that, okay? No matter what happens, you're already one of the lucky ones."

I remember Yeon-Jae. Why does everyone keep saying I'm lucky? She must wish she knew her parents too. I watch her stride out the door and when I turn back around, Joe is standing up behind the counter, staring at me with wide eyes.

"Arthur? Arthur!" He waves me close, and when I get to the counter, talks under his breath. "Holy shit, your sister is worried sick about you, man! Where have you been?"

"I, uh ... I decided to join up." I shrug. "Like you did."

"What?" I'm surprised to see his eye twitch speed up until he pins it down with a finger. "Why the hell would you do that?"

"I'm almost 20. I'm taking care of myself now."

"Is that why?" Joe points to the box and his expression is guarded.

A weight settles on my shoulders as I set the burden on the counter. "No, but I'm glad it worked out."

"They just gave you the ashes?" Joe looks stunned as he rubs the back of his neck.

"Yeah. I said I needed them for closure ... Can you get them to Gina? Don't tell her you got them from me though, okay? I don't want her to know I joined yet."

"Arthur, you need to tell her. She's losing it, man." Joe scowls at me.

"You're such a hypocrite! I'm just doing what you did." Why do I feel like I have to defend myself? "You wouldn't have this job if you hadn't joined up."

"I know." Joe sighs.

"I'm doing great, Joe, I swear. Way better than back home. I just ... I don't want to fight with her right now."

"But she's losing her mind, man." Joe rubs at his eye. "You just up and disappeared."

"Fine. You can tell her you saw me. Just ... say I needed to get away for a while. Can you send her the ashes so somehow it looks like the Community sent them?"

"Yeah, kid. Alright."

"I'm not a kid. I'm a customer." I smile and hold my hand out, ignoring the nerves twisting my guts.

"Really?" Joe asks, sticking his tongue in his cheek. "Let's see how much you got." Joe scans my hand and my new wetware connection shows the balance of my small account on his countertop. "Yeah, this could get you a couple of services." He still looks unhappy.

"I'm going to talk to her once I'm settled in, I swear. Then I can take care of both of us. Gina can still live off-GRID if she wants. She won't have to kill herself trying to take care of me on her own."

"Look, kid. There are things at play right now that you don't understand." Joe leans across the counter and whispers. "I swear to God I'm not bullshitting you. This isn't just about your sister. You have got to be more careful than you've ever been in your whole life."

"What do you mean?"

"I can get you a meeting with some pretty important people if you can give me a couple of days. But you've got to swear to me. Don't tell anybody. Don't tell that AI. No one."

"You're not talking about squids or something are you?" A chill runs down my spine from even mentioning the terrorist organization. Just who the hell is Joe in with now?

"No man," he sighs. "They're people connected to your family. People from North Continent. They have information about your parents."

"Mom and Dad?" I choke. "You'd better not be—"

"I'm supposed to watch out for you." He's still pinning his eye down. "I know you feel all alone right now, but you aren't. You've got to promise me that you'll come talk to them and hear them out. Please."

"When? How will I even know?"

"Two days. Just two days and I swear they'll be here. You can meet me right here at the counter."

"Fine. You don't have to be so dramatic."

"Good. Just be careful, and don't leave Gina hangin' too long." Joe swallows hard. "Now. Go pick out a girl and we'll get you a room. I won't tell your sister."

CHAPTER
8

The next day, Manuela pops up as I'm brushing my teeth in the bathroom. "How are you feeling this morning, Arthur?"

"Okay." I try to rub the stiffness out of my neck. Damn Joe had to go and stress me out. Who the hell from North Continent would still know my parents?

"Are you still benefiting from your medication?"

"Yeah, it's fine." I spit out my toothpaste and rinse my mouth out. "Why? What's up?"

"Today is a very big day." Her smile is smaller than normal.

"What does that mean?" I laugh and turn toward her as I dry my hands. "And what's up with you? I didn't think AIs had down days."

"I never know what to expect from humans during transitions. You are all so different."

"What are you saying?"

She flips instantly to a radiant smile. "Today is your first day of server duty. And your first day of transitioning into permanent housing."

"Oh." Wow. Thank God I got Mom and Dad's ashes to Joe yesterday. That must have been why she was pestering me. "Well, that's great! Manni ... I'm excited about this. I want to see how well I can support ..." Gina. "Myself. You know? I've never been able to do that before."

"Of course." She nods with a smile. "I have directions here to the server bank where you will be connected for the first time."

"Is it different from where they tested my connection?" I walk to the display screen in the bedroom.

"You don't need the mirror, silly. You can pull up the GRID interface just by thinking about it now."

"Oh, yeah." I decide to close my eyes, so it's not as disorienting. Whoa. This is awesome. Wait. "Holy crap. Why the hell is it so far away? Aren't there server banks close to here?"

"There are," she says, appearing in my mind this time, "but this one is closer to your final placement."

"What about my medicine?"

"They will have that ready for you when you arrive."

"Manni, be honest." I sigh. "How is my connection doing? Does it lag because of the EDS?"

"Are you experiencing any anomalies?"

"No, nothing on my end. I just really want this to work."

"Honestly, Arthur, you are a star performer. We'll have to see more with a longer-term session, but so far your processing speed is above average."

"Awesome. It's nice to finally be good at something. Should I pack up my stuff?"

"No need. Your belongings will be transferred for you, just as before."

"Okay. Great." I grab my assigned jacket and head out the door.

After taking an autobus all the way to District F, I get off at the job site. The buildings seem ominous, huge and black. A cold shiver runs down my spine.

Don't be a baby. Get Mom out of your head. Joe was just freakin' you out.

Whoa, the buildings here are at least 40 stories tall! They form some kind of giant complex. The glass on their exterior is a flat black and I can't see anything inside.

I summon my courage with a deep breath and walk through the front doors. The overhead speaker announces my arrival. I've gotten used to buildings registering my CID when I walk in over the last few days. For such an enormous building, the waiting room is incredibly small. All four chairs look uncomfortable, but I don't get a chance to sit down.

"This way," a short brunette in gray scrubs says after appearing from a door to my right.

"Okay." I try to sound confident. "Manuela said that you guys have my meds?"

"We'll get you taken care of." She smiles.

I jump slightly when I hear the door click loudly behind us. You think I'd be used to that from Manuela, but this feels different.

Wow, Mom's done a number on me.

I'm led into a small server room. Two other people are already here—walking along on treadmills with empty expressions. This looks like what I expected. I've heard about this. They're run on an exercise program while the GRID borrows their brains for a bit.

"Am I starting work today?"

"Yes. The doctor will be right with you." She leaves and I stand awkwardly in the room with the dead-eyed workers.

The doctor that comes in is a huge, dark-skinned man in really dark purple scrubs. He looks grim. "Good morning, Arthur." He holds a hand out toward the treadmill. "Step on up for me."

When I do, he hooks patient monitors to my chest and a silicone pad to my cheek—like when they tested my connection speed. I take an instinctive step back when a needle on a robotic arm extends from the wall in front of me.

"No need to be afraid." He resists my flight with a hand on my back.

"What's that for?"

"It's just going to run an IV line. We don't want you to get dehydrated."

I swallow down my fear as I let the machine connect me to the IV system, but I start to feel panicky. This isn't right! Lots of people have told me what working at the servers is like. No one ever mentioned an IV.

"We're going to start your session now. Do you have any questions?"

"How long is my shift? I didn't get my meds yet."

"That depends on how you do," he says, getting that glassy-eyed look. "No need to worry. We'll run your medications through the IV, and you won't remember anything from your session. You'll just feel like you're waking up when it's over."

That didn't answer my question. I'm about to ask again when he activates the program.

CHAPTER
9

I feel myself drift in and out of consciousness over and over again. People's hands are always on me, and sometimes I can hear voices. I try to fight my way back, but I can't wake up.

Finally, I hear a soft, steady beeping noise. I feel small tubes connected to my face, pushing air up my nose, and when I try to move, it seems like more are taped to my arms. I open my eyes and they feel like they're full of sand. I have to squint because the light is way too bright. My body feels heavy and strangely numb.

This isn't right! Server duty isn't like this! People wake up and walk off feeling good. They do it every day. Panic begins rising in my throat, and I struggle to sit up. The beeping beside me increases its pace.

"Calm down, Arthur," a woman whispers in a gentle voice. "Everything's alright. Just take your time."

That's not Manuela's voice.

"Who are you?" What happened to my voice?

"I'm Dr. Chase." She turns my face with her hand so I can see her. Her face is pleasant above her dark purple scrubs, but her eyes look tired.

"What happened? Where am I?"

"You're in Institution 231 for disabled citizens."

An institution? Wait ... "Why?"

"Oh come now, Arthur," she says with a sigh. "I know your condition was explained to you. The treatment the Community provides you is designed to ease your suffering, but it is also very costly. You need a variety of daily medications, physical therapy exercises, and assistive technology. Naturally, your own contribution needs to be a little bit more than the average citizen. You'll be allowed to take breaks from your service here in your room and have some time for yourself."

I glance wildly around the room. I'm lying in a hospital bed. The room has a small desk with a single chair on one side—the chair she is sitting on. There is a small locker in the corner, and a window I can't possibly fit through. I pat my hands past what seems like leads on my chest, and then—What's happened to my stomach? My hands bump into something hard, and I cry out in surprise and pain.

"Be careful." She stands to force my hands back down to my sides. "You don't want to damage your feeding tube."

"How long? How long have I been hooked to that machine?" How long has Gina been waiting for me?

"Your session lasted three months and seven days. Your brain performs wonderfully." She turns off the sound of my racing pulse.

Three months!

"I want to leave. Please. Let me go." I sob. My voice is weak and pitiful.

"We can't do that," the crazy lady says. "Your health is much too poor to be out on your own. You're making a fine contribution to your Community right here."

"No!" I start pushing her hands away. "No, I don't need this. I have to find my sister!"

"Sister?" she whispers and backs up against the door. "Arthur, I have to ask you to calm yourself. I know it can be a difficult adjustment."

"Get out of my way!" Cursing my weakness, I try to push myself off the bed.

I don't see her move.

Sharp pain flares in the side of my neck, and I look up to see that she's shoved something against it. I swat it out of her hand, and what bounces across the floor looks like a miniature injector. With all my strength, I arch my back and roll out of bed onto my feet. I lean forward and stumble out into the hallway. My legs feel heavy and my brain can't seem to tell them what to do.

Stumbling, I collapse onto the floor. I roll onto my side and try to push myself back up, but I can't.

She's dosed me with something!

"Pick him up." I hear the woman's tired voice behind me. "This one's going to be difficult. He said something about family. Make double sure his record is thoroughly sterilized and prep him for another transfer. Well, hurry up! Before he damages something!"

Two huge men lift me and drop me back into the bed in the tiny cell.

"Please," I sob, but it comes out slurred. "Please let me go home."

One of the men looks down at me with a sad expression. "You are home, kid."

Turn the page for a sneak peek at the next title in
The Infinitus Saga.

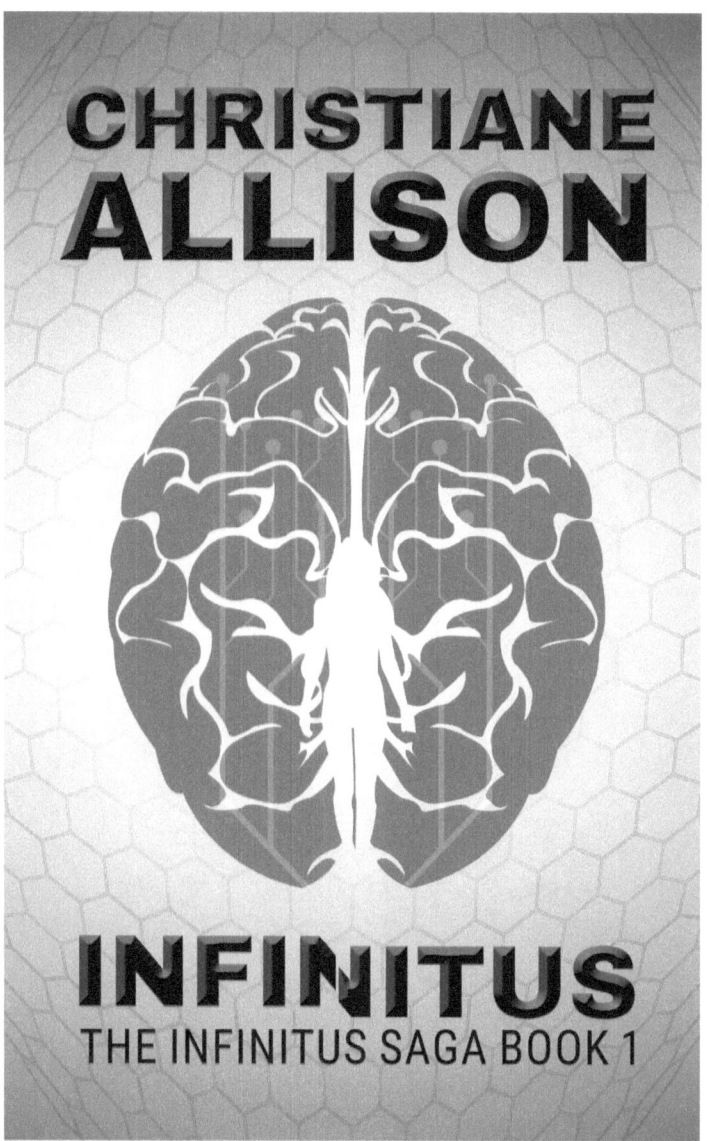

Available now from Allison Publishing!

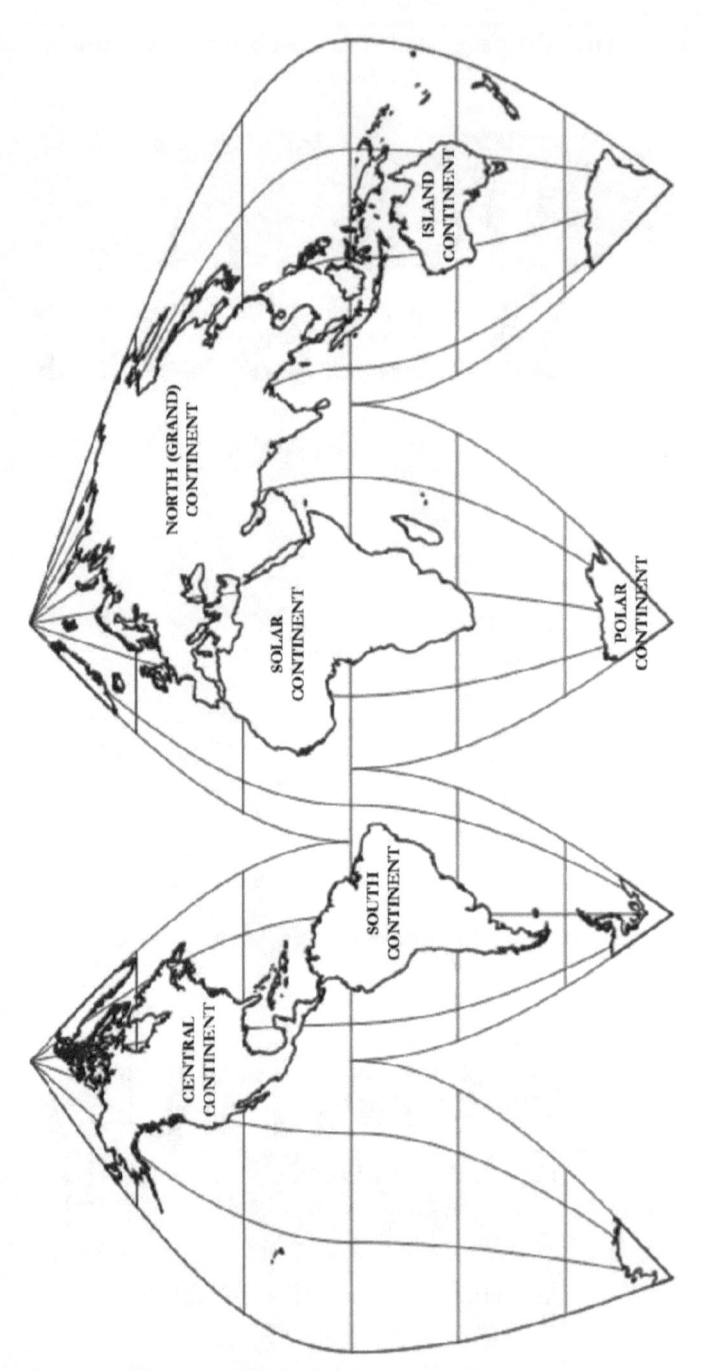

PROLOGUE

September 24

North Continent, Region 130, Sector 26, District M

Fifty-six tables is a massive showing. The defiant statement a meet this size makes to the Global Fellowship has me uneasy, even this many stories underground. Every year that passes, the black market traders lose some of their fear that shields will step in and shut them down. It would help if the Community didn't need the markets as much as the dealers do.

"Hey, Jared!" Kegan shouts from two tables over. "Nice to see you in sector, man. Come over here!"

I nod and saunter through the crowd. "What's up?" I ask. "You have something worth seeing?"

Kegan is a little guy, only about five-foot-six, and chronically wired on caffeine and amphetamines. One of these days, his heart will explode, and he'll drop dead. I hope I'm not there for that. "I'm telling you," he says, rubbing his hands together, "I've got a great systems update for your med pods."

"What kind of update?"

He launches into his sales pitch. Within a couple of lines, I can tell I got it months ago. He's got nothing I need.

Normally, I'm here to offload tech the Community doesn't want to take a loss on while using my front as a tech dealer to gather intel from these underworld powerhouses. This time, I have another assignment. It's not every day I'm given someone to purchase. I look for that myself.

Word on the street spread quickly that there's a chimera up for sale. One whose animal traits will be deadly in the wrong hands. I'm bringing them in for a memory reset, which would be a lot easier to do if my handler gave me any information at all about the chimera they're looking for. The lazy ass just expects me to sniff them out.

Faking continued interest for Kegan's benefit, I pull a rolled-up flex out of my pocket and scroll through the items I have for trade. The smart glass is starting to crease. I'll have to replace it soon. Looking around, the expansive room is filled to the brim with dealers and their goods, walls gleaming with silver Faraday paint.

I'm not sure where to start, but after drawing the scent of the market in, a subtle, unpleasant musk catches my attention. I turn my head to search for the source. It's reptilian. The scent is four tables down, drifting from a shipping crate you'd use for a large dog.

"What's with the crate?" I ask.

Kegan usually sticks his nose, and anything else he can, into his neighbors' business. "Man, I'd steer clear of that shit," he says with a low whistle. "I don't see why people don't just get their poison from snakes. It's gotta be diluted with the human genetics, you know?"

"Huh," I say, keeping my shoulders from tensing. "I'm gonna check it out."

Ignoring Kegan's continued protests, I approach the booth. My hands are secured in my pockets to resist strangling the booth's dealer if there really is a person shoved in that tiny aluminum box. When the dealer finally wanders back over, I recognize her—blond, short, curvy, and always wearing six-inch stilettos she could kill with. She's a titanium arms dealer, newly upgraded from stainless. "Hey Juanita," I call with a smile. "What's with the crate? You selling exotic pets now?"

"Oh, this is no pet." She cranes her neck to look up at me. "Have we met before?"

"Jared." Extending my hand, I combat the urge to crush her smaller, softer one. "Just a platinum dealer, but I'm always looking for a way up."

"Well honey, this is your formula, right here."

The stench that hits me as she pulls back the crate's window curtain makes me nauseous. The person inside is definitely a chimera. In fact, he has genetics I understand extremely well.

He's got ebony skin with cream-colored scales above his eyebrows, beneath his mouth, and peeking out under his shirt along his collar bones. He's not a man. He's a kid. I'm not around kids much, so I'm not sure, but I'd size him as over ten and under thirteen years.

So, this is the big, bad, venomous chimera everyone is so freaked out about? This kid wouldn't even be out of training yet if he'd been raised like me. He was probably abandoned by his birth mother. Well ... unless he bit her.

The kid's eyes are hollow in a way I'm all too familiar with. Now focusing on my face, his head cocks sideways slightly as he draws a deep breath. Keep it cool, kid. I wink at him. No giving away my secrets with that nose of yours. He shrinks back into the shadows of the crate.

"How much you asking?" I cover the crate back up.

"Three million coin."

Hawking's Ghost! She can't be serious. Kegan spews some colorful language behind me. If his heart doesn't explode, one of these dealers is going to shoot him for listening in on the wrong deal.

"Come on. Be real, Juanita," I say. "How many people have the connections to use an opportunity like this? I do and I'm standing here. I'll give you two million."

Kegan walks up, leaving his partner at his table. "What in the Universe are you going to do with a chimera?"

"Sell him to an elite." I shrug. "What else?" I wish that elite wasn't Alex.

Juanita runs her tongue over her teeth and glances around the market, taking in who else may come to the table. "Two and a half."

"Two and a quarter, or I won't even make a profit on him. No one else will either. Don't push your luck." I make a subtle show that I've caught sight of another interesting prospect. "I'll come by later."

"You've got a deal." Juanita gives a half-hearted shrug, but her eyes are pleased. Finally, she passes over her flex.

2

GINA

Same Day
Central Continent, Region 84, Sector 10, District T

"Gina." Tommy's rich, deep voice calls me out of my tortured thoughts. "Sweetheart, you haven't moved in over an hour. I'd be hard-pressed to catch you blinkin'."

Tommy leans down on his elbows, bringing his concerned black eyes level with mine. His armbands, tattooed on his enormous biceps in bright white, black light ink, stand out starkly against his ebony skin and black t-shirt. I hate making him worry.

"Sorry." Lifting my moonshine daiquiri—What the heck? I'm out?—I scoot the glass toward Tommy and tap the rim, glancing away.

"You can't mean that." His eyebrows wrinkle together with concern. "Girl, that's already your third. Is your pain really that bad?"

The question brings a knife-like sensation to my chest and I struggle to breathe. In seconds, traitorous tears spill down my cheeks. Dammit. I don't want to make a spectacle of myself.

"Shit." Tommy heads for his backroom.

I shouldn't even be here. I knew I couldn't sing my normal gig today—not tomorrow either. Stress amplifies my chronic pain—a lovely little symptom called fibromyalgia that sets my nervous system on fire. As bad as it is, though, it's nothing compared to the pain in my heart.

One year ago today, my parents died in a horrific autocab accident.

God help me. Another assault of bloody images arises from my memory as a shudder runs through me. Rob warned me. I shouldn't have looked, but I couldn't stop myself.

Five days later, my nineteen-year-old little brother disappeared. He was too weak and fragile to have made it alone. He was always so much sicker than me, and the shock of Mom and Dad's death made both of us so much worse. He wouldn't have been able to carry anything or walk far. He never could leave home for more than an hour or two, and he had zero experience with how to stay safe.

My mind starts to spin with all the ways he could have been killed or hurt along the way … No! No. He wouldn't have attempted it unless he knew he could get to Drustan, our missing older brother. Which means, Drustan must have heard about the accident.

But why didn't they wait for me?

The problem is, I have no idea how to find them. My parents were our only link to Drustan, and they took that information with them in death. So here I sit, using moonshine to dull my sorrow, still hoping that someday Drustan and Arthur will come for me.

"Here ya go," Tommy says.

He sets a new daiquiri down on the bar and I take a deep drink, ignoring the combination of chill and burn.

"If ya drink much more of that"—Tommy frowns—"I'm gonna have to call you an autocab. I'll pay for it."

I choke on the drink, recoiling from the suggestion so severely I nearly topple from the barstool. Tommy reaches over the bar, grabbing my shoulders to steady me.

"Sweet baby Einstein! What on Earth was that about, girl?"

"I don't … want a c-cab."

"Do you really think you're gonna walk all the way back down to the Dregs like this? I could just ..." Understanding dawns in his eyes before he closes them momentarily. He probably pulled up his calendar interface. "Aw shit Doll, I'm sorry. I didn't even think when you asked for the day off. I should've realized then."

"It doesn't matter." A wave of dizziness catches me by surprise so I lay my head on the bar.

"Does it still hurt after all this time?" He gently strokes my hair.

"It will—every year."

"Then come on to the back."

Tommy comes to my side of the bar, sliding his strong, dark arm around my waist to pull me from my seat. "What ... doing? I can't sing."

"Girl, that's obvious." He laughs and I appreciate the rich sound. My father used to laugh like that. "But ya drink much more and you're not gonna be sitting in that chair either. Ya gonna be lying on the floor."

Tommy helps me into the tiny dressing room in back and sets me down on the futon. I lie down, battling a new wave of dizziness as he brushes my hair back from my face. The weight of a thin blanket settles across my body. "I'm sorry," he whispers. "I didn't know your OAS was so bad. I don't know how to help ya without a doc."

OAS—Obsessive Attachment Syndrome. Glancing at Tommy's face, my heart sinks further as I acknowledge his belief that my condition is a mental illness, the most feared mental illness in the Community. "I'm not sick."

"Girl." He sighs. "How can ya look at yourself right now and say that? You've worked for me for six years now and I haven't ever seen ya in pain like this—except a year ago."

Tommy is like most people in the world. He didn't know his parents—or siblings, if he had any. After he left University, his birth mother did track him down, but only to pass along the moonshiner tradition—their little rebellion in a world where alcohol is illegal. She didn't stick around. He lives the typical life: unattached, unobsessed, and perfectly healthy according to everyone else.

"You don't know what you're missing. If I could have them all back today, I'd take 'em."

"You still believe those brothers are coming for ya?"

"No." The truth slips past my lips. Weak. Traitor. Fraud.

"Well, then they a couple of fools." Tommy brushes my hair back again. "If ya gonna break the rules, ya might as well break it for something pretty and smart. With those green-brown eyes and that heart that holds ya tight."

Careful, Tommy. You're going to develop OAS yourself. We can't have that.

"Where is that man of yours anyway? He should be loving ya and taking your mind off all those attachments that been hurting so hacking bad."

Ah yes. My ever-present imaginary boyfriend and primary excuse. No one understands a desire for monogamous love, and they understand chastity even less. I may as well declare that I dance around altars and sacrifice fluffy bunny rabbits to a herd of unicorns. "Delivery. Out of town."

"Bad timing if ya ask me. I tell ya what, Doll. You just stay back here and sleep for the night. You can start that long walk home in the morning. After all, we don't want our moonshine secret found passed out on the street now."

"Fine—I mean … thanks." The nerve pain is starting to flare back to life in my legs. I won't be able to work tomorrow anyway.

3

HAWK

September 25
North Continent, Region 109, Sector 4, District A

The hotel room is freezing, so I close my eyes and mentally pull up GRID access. Instantly, I'm standing by the pond in the nicest park mid-sector—a standard hotel menu theme.

"Good evening, Jared," Manuela says as she walks up beside me in the mental landscape. "What are your needs?" She always appears exactly the same with highlighted black hair, brown eyes, and bronzed skin. I could change her up if I want, but never interact with her long enough to deal with it.

"Just help me with the room. It's like a bogon fridge in here." I reopen my eyes, abandoning the mental menu since Manuela can do it for me. She projects herself into the room through my mind. I need to seal up for security and prepare the environment for the chimera's unique needs. "Raise the temperature to 72 degrees. Lights on full."

"Adjusting settings now. How was your trip?"

"It was normal." I begin a full security sweep of the room. There's nothing under the queen bed or nightstand.

"Are you upset?"

"No." Even though I only use this identity sporadically, Manuela should have learned by now that I don't make small talk with AI. The hall closet and bathroom are empty. "I'm fine."

"My sensors indicate there are no additional people inside this room."

"Yeah." And your sensors can be tricked. "I just …"

"I know you like to check," she says with a smile. "Would you like me to order entertainment for you?"

There's no left-behind tech beneath the small table in the corner or the two wooden chairs. "No. I want to sleep and not be disturbed in any way."

"I do not have the ability to override emergency alerts."

Glancing out the balcony door, my exact drone delivery instructions were followed. Thank Science for quality control protocols. The crate is on the balcony beneath a heat-shield, to keep the boy cool and hamper both curious eyes and Manuela's body heat sensors. The kid came with samples of the venom he produces, and I received confirmation during hyperloop travel that the antivenoms I carry for Cobra should be effective against the brunt of it. Not that I'm going to let him bite me.

"Manuela, tint the windows to 100 percent. I need to sleep."

"Tinting now. Would you like a hot bath?"

"Not tonight. Leave only emergency protocols active. Activate Do Not Disturb."

"Very well, Jared. Have a good night. I will be here when you need me."

I glance at the entry panel to confirm her disconnect, then activate my signal jammer, sealing the room. The balcony door opens with a slight hiss as I approach.

"Instructions?" the crate's cheap voice says, sensing my movement.

A thorough scan of the surrounding area doesn't turn up any problems. There are two people on a balcony on the building across from this one, but they're in some kind of heated discussion. Neither of them have bulges in their clothing that would indicate weapons. None of the street cams have direct angles on this room. At street level the autocabs and pedestrians are moving steadily except for a young mother struggling with her flailing infant, who has spotted the stray cat around the corner. I don't see any nosy people or drones. "Enter."

"Authorization?" the crate asks.

"Jared Altrax, confirm CID. Security code 9-2-4-Bravo-Delta-Tango-6-2-Charlie. Confirmation Azure-Epsilon-Granite."

"Authorization confirmed." Wheels emerge from the crate's bottom before it steers itself inside. After the door shuts, I flip the switch to disconnect its power supply.

I've got incredible hearing, but the kid inside isn't making any sound aside from breathing. "Hey, kid." I tap on the crate's aluminum top. "You still alive in there?"

He doesn't respond so I pull the heat-shield off and drop down, looking through the thin front bars. Two wide, terrified eyes gaze back at me. Hawking's ghost, he smells awful. "Do you speak English?"

He nods.

"Did the food and water I put in there last?"

He nods again.

"Look, kid." I sigh, sitting down to face the crate. "I'm sorry you've been stuck in that shit hole this whole time, but it was the best way to get you here. I'd like to let you out, but you've got to convince me that you're not gonna bite me the second I open this door."

He blinks a few times but otherwise doesn't move.

"You got a name?"

I'm surprised when he shakes his head. I didn't expect that answer.

"What about one you like? Something you want to be called?"

He's quiet for a long time, tilting his head this way and that. Finally he whispers, "Human."

"Sorry, kid. No one's gonna mistake you for that, but I can help you live a life outside this box if you want."

"You can?" The boy leans forward to grab the bars. "You look like them, but smell like me. You are like me."

Hack, this kid's nose is one in a trillion. I need to know just how sensitive it is. "What do I smell like?"

"Snake. Cat. Bird." He tips his head. "There's more, but it's too mixed up."

"Good nose. What about you? What's in your genes?"

He shrugs. "Snake. Spider. Something from the sea. Everything bad."

"Why don't you have a name?"

"I don't know."

"Do you remember your birth mother?"

"They said she was dead—said I did it."

Shit. Humans can be cruel. "Well, no pressure. You pick a name when you want. Till then, I'll stick with kid. Is that alright?"

He nods, then his eyes settle where his hands grip the bars. "Why don't they put you in a box?"

"They decided I'm more useful outside of one. I do a ton of important work, including buying kids that shouldn't be in boxes."

I wish I could look this kid in the eye and tell him life is great on this side of the bars, that he has amazing things to look forward to. Reality sucks. We're all confined by the roles we fit, but at least we're not aimless or exploited.

The retirement ad I saw last week made me wish I had options like everyone else. I could make an appointment, walk in, tell them I don't want to keep going, and they'd put me to sleep for good. It's painless and your body's recycled.

The Community would never let that happen though. They've already freaked out enough to put me on pills, which I can't take and do my job. I'm a well-trained, highly-skilled asset. They need me to do this kind of work because there aren't enough of us to do it. "Can I trust you not to bite me, if I let you out?"

"Yeah." He tucks his chin down to his chest. "I didn't mean to hurt anybody."

When I open the crate, the kid takes his time unfolding. I can tell it causes him pain. An hour later, I'm able to coax him up to the table by eating in front of him with a second bowl out, acting as casual about the food as I can. He starts asking questions about my work, so I explain my role in the Community to him while he eats. If he works extra hard, he might be able to catch up to the other chimera kids his age, or pass them. Then he can get into work like mine. It's not the best future, but it's a lot better than life in a box.

The chime from the door startles us both. For Tesla's sake, how long have we been talking? The kid dives back inside the crate before my eyes have even closed to pull up the feed from the external cam. It's who I expect. I wish I could avoid seeing him, but I walk over and manually open the door.

Alex steps through wearing an ivory silk shirt and brown dress slacks that I'm sure conceal thin body armor beneath. I hate how much of his face looks back at me in the mirror every morning—the sharp jaw and strong nose of western North Continent look more natural with his paler skin and brown hair.

Despite contributing half my DNA, Alex is a Community elite, a respected scientist. Instead of being ashamed of my genetics, he revels in what I am. He chose to be the lead researcher for all global chimera units. If only he had a human soul. "This is the boy?" Alex asks after the door closes. "Why in Tesla's name is he still in that crate?"

"Because you startled us."

"Startled you?" Alex scoffs. "Keep your mind on your work. The child's needs aren't something for you to deal with."

I decide not to argue and scare the kid more. "He doesn't have a name. I told him I would just call him kid for now."

"Thus, you don't work with children."

"Whatever, Alex." He hates it when I call him that. "Are you going to help him or not?"

"Obviously. Young man, come out here so we can get moving." Shitty thing is, Alex is the one who should never be trusted with children. The man is a sociopath, but he's my only option.

"Come on, kid." I sit on the floor by the crate to get back on his level. "You've got to go with Alex now."

The kid pokes his head out past the door, and he has tears on his face.

"He's not gonna hurt you." I hope that's the truth.

"I want to stay with you," the kid says, wiping his tears. "I can help you. I know I can."

"I'm sorry. That's not an option. They're going to give you a new life. Let you start over. You'd like a new life, right? You'd like to be like me?"

"But I don't want to forget you!" The kid suddenly sobs.

Alex jerks his head back and raises an eyebrow. "You told him about the memory wipe?"

"Of course I did. He's had enough people lie to him. It's not going to hurt him to know what to expect. He'll forget the pain when he forgets the rest of it."

"No please!" The kid bursts out of the shipping container and nearly knocks me over when he jumps in my lap. "Please, Jared! I want to stay with you!"

"Hey, hey, whoa." I wish I had the right words to calm him. "It's not going to be what you imagine, kid." I run my fingers lightly through his hair, feeling oddly peaceful from this sense of connection to someone I barely know.

I saw a birth mother do this at a commissary once for a much smaller child, and I remember wishing I'd had a mother who'd done that for me. My mother couldn't wait to turn me over. She put me into Alex's questionable care on the day I was born. I have no memories of being held.

"What do you mean?" The kid continues crying.

"Right now, you remember being stuck in that sick box," I say. "You remember all the people who've been cruel to you. Maybe I seem like something special, but it's only because you've spent your whole life being treated like shit. Sure, after the memory wipe you won't remember me." The thought makes my throat tight, but I cough it away. "But you won't remember the shitheads either. You'll be able to start over. Clean slate. You'll get the respect you earn, and you'll meet new people who'll treat you with the respect an operative deserves."

"You promise?"

I glance up at Alex and, of course, he has no reassurance to offer. "Yeah, kid," I say. "I promise."

The next time I think about retirement, I'll just remember what happens to these kids without me. Better than pills any day.

LEAVE A REVIEW

Dear reader,

Did you enjoy <u>The Global Fellowship</u> and the sneak peek of <u>Infinitus</u>? Sign up for my newsletter at www.AllisonPublishing.com to stay informed about the release of Infinitus, other new releases, author signings, and exciting news. You can even find my personal playlist for The Global Fellowship when you visit:

www.AllisonPublishing.com/books#/the-global-fellowship

While you're there, please leave a quick review for this book. The more honest reviews I have, the more readers will see my book and know if it's one they'd like to read. Here's an easy link:

http://smarturl.it/rev_GlobalFellowship

Thank you for helping me out!

ABOUT THE AUTHOR

Photo © 2018 Liz Shine

Christiane Joy Allison is a multi-award-winning author, activist, and public speaker. She lives with her sprawling, loving family in the beautiful state of Alaska. Living with Ehlers-Danlos Syndrome (hEDS), she understands the struggle of disability.

In 2018, Christiane was the proud recipient of both a Rasmuson Foundation Individual Artist Project Award and an Alaska Writers Guild Lin Halterman Memorial Grant. Her first children's picture book won five honorable mentions in the 2018 Purple Dragonfly Book Awards. She's making her debut in dystopian science-fiction with this series. You can connect with her at:

www.AllisonPublishing.com
www.Facebook.com/ChristianeJoyAllison
Twitter.com/CJAllison7
www.Instagram.com/ChristianeJoyAllison
Amazon.com/author/ChristianeJoyAllison